The Chronicles of
Lord Asunaro

Kanji Hanawa

A former professor of French literature with an interest in human psychology and complex relationships, Hanawa's narratives expose the pressures and challenges of life in Japan.

Hanawa is a master of the short story. He has written several hundred since he published his first collection, *Garasu no natsu* (*Glass Summer*) to critical acclaim in 1972.

In 1962, after graduating from Tokyo University, where he studied French Literature, he spent several months in Pau and Paris, his only stay in the country to whose literature he has dedicated much of his life.

Since retiring from academic life (having translated into Japanese 15 novels by some of France's most eminent authors and researching the works of the French poet Arthur Rimbaud), he now lives in Tokyo with his wife and son. He is at last completely free to dedicate himself to his real passion: writing short stories about life in ancient, modern and contemporary Japan.

Two of his novellas have been shortlisted for the prestigious Akutagawa Prize.

Translator: Meredith McKinney

Meredith McKinney has translated numerous works of Japanese literature, from the earliest poetry to contemporary fiction. Among them are classics such as *The Pillow Book*, as well as Natsume Soseki's early modern masterpiece *Kokoro*, and an anthology of a thousand years of classical Japanese travel writing (*Travels with a Writing Brush*). She lives in the bush outside the small town of Braidwood in New South Wales.

Also by Kanji Hanawa in English translation
Compos Mentis
Backlight

A full publication list of all of Hanawa's work is available from
www.redcircleauthors.com

The Chronicles of
Lord Asunaro

Kanji Hanawa

Translated from the Japanese by
Meredith McKinney

Red Circle

Published by Red Circle Authors Limited
First edition 2020
1 3 5 7 9 10 8 6 4 2

Red Circle Authors Limited
Third Floor, 24 Chiswell Street,
London EC1Y 4YX

Red Circle
www.redcircleauthors.com

Design by Aiko Ishida, typesetting by Danny Lyle
Set in Adobe Caslon Pro

ISBN: 978-1-912864-06-5

A catalogue record of this book is available from the British Library.

In memory of Sanjiro Hanawa (1897–1962),
my father, the Chief Justice of the
Tokyo Court of Appeal.

The Chronicles of
Lord Asunaro

The Education of
Young Asunaro

Every morning, the young son of a certain feudal lord was woken at a fixed hour when the doors and paper screens of his bedroom were drawn open, in undeviating order and with the same predictable clatter. Impassively and regardless of the weather, his gaze fell first on the tasteful courtyard garden beyond the window.

Next, his eyes lifted to the lowest roof of the corner tower and began to count off through the pine branches the round eave tiles, their gold leaf flaking in patches, before he gave up half way as he always did. Thus did the young lord of the West Castle commence his day.

Lord though he was in name, not one important task in the governance of the domain ever came his way, despite his having reached maturity. He still vividly recalled the childhood experience of living with his father, the current lord. His father would be seated with weighty formality in the room where official business was conducted, running his eye over the documents that his personal attendants bustled to and fro to bring him, their socked feet brushing the floor with each obsequious step, and passing personal judgement or adding notes to what his secretary had recorded there. Strenuous work though it seemed, to the young boy's eyes it all appeared to proceed with seamless ease.

From time to time the atmosphere in the castle underwent a radical change, a bevy of senior retainers came pouring in, and the secretary and others were dismissed. Safely hidden, the boy alone stayed on, peering out through a crack between the sliding doors of the neighbouring room.

There had been unprecedented flooding rains in the domain, he understood, and this meeting was to deal with the problem.

'You're telling me this is the state things have reached in my domain? What am I to make of this, now that matters are at such a pass?'

The lord's shrill voice belied his age. While the retainers bent their little white-haired topknots together in huddled conference he alone remained erect, head held high.

'Unfortunately there has been heavy flooding throughout the domain this year, your lordship, and there is almost total devastation, particularly in the lowland area's fields that produce good quality rice, and almost all of the fields that produce our finest rice.'

'Hmm. So I suppose this means we must distribute our stockpiles of rice throughout the domain, even down to the farmers.' The declaration was self-consciously in the style of The Benevolent Ruler.

'If they heard of that, my lord, some in the castle would say, "You mean we samurai can be left to starve to death? Surely it doesn't matter how many farmers die?"'

'Don't be ridiculous! If the commoners' anger turns to riot, the central government will hear of it and it would be nothing short of disaster, just as happened in that other domain, remember? No, we must all tighten our belts here. No luxuries from now on, even for the women and children.'

'Hey there, young master! You've been listening to this, have you? Well just make sure you don't breathe a word of it, *ho ho ho…*'

A lady-in-waiting quickly hustled the boy away. This he did remember, but thereafter any such matters were always conducted out of his earshot. The answer to why he was thus excluded can be found in a certain ancient tome, essentially a kind of performance report on the feudal lords of the time, in which our young lord is candidly described as 'a fool from birth, and lacking all judgement'.

The long period of warfare that had preceded this time did not come to any sudden resounding end, like some great door slamming shut, but lingered fractiously on for a while longer. Nevertheless, no domain was untouched by painful struggles in this time of transition from a wartime mentality to one of peace.

In this domain, as elsewhere, there was a pressing need to rectify the haphazard finances that had characterised the previous age when warfare was the norm. Enforcing frugality on the retainers necessitated merciless punishment of those who resisted. In such matters we catch a glimpse of the age's cruelty. But thanks to these brutal remedies the finances of the domain did indeed recover, all were loud in the lord's praise, and there were even some who numbered him among the four top rulers in the land.

'This will surely have made you a Forebear, your lordship,' declared one of his senior vassals. To 'become a Forebear' was to be deemed one whose name would wield retrospective authority, as in the admiring phrase 'his forebear was so-and-so, you know'. Be it for teachings, fame, erudition or military prowess, if those who heard one's name shrank in awe then one was effectively a Forebear. This being no mean feat, you would imagine that modesty should prevent a man from acknowledging it of himself, but his lordship felt no such qualms.

'You think so? Well for good or ill, there's no stopping people's tongues from wagging I suppose, *haw haw haw*.'

His generally unsmiling countenance looked far from displeased. And sure enough, in the aforementioned ancient tome he is indeed recorded as being 'renowned for both his literary and military skills'.

Yet this is not to say that no cares clouded his life. Seated before his vassals in conference, he would assume a relaxed air and encourage them to feel free to say whatever they liked, but not one word broke the general hush. Once a youthful voice from the dim recesses of the back row was heard to produce the following frank response:

'But your lordship, if I may be so bold, the chamber so brims with the force of your esteemed presence that none of the foregathered has the courage to open his mouth.'

Thunderstruck, all those present tensed still more rigidly. His lordship was across every aspect of things, and whatever was said to him threatened to rebound on the speaker with interest; his ugly pockmarked face was an intimidating sight, and everyone flinched at what this utterance might provoke. Happily, however, he merely smiled grimly and chose to remain silent.

Thanks to the favour of The Supreme One (as the great Shogun Ieyasu Tokugawa was known), his lordship's possession of the domain was secure – no doubt in reward for that admirable love of his not only for fighting but for learning. Along the walls of his library there towered a great cone-shaped mountain of bound books.

Since his realm continued thus unthreatened, his lordship was in no position to complain. There were times, however, when the question of a successor troubled him. Perhaps the son he pinned his hopes on would die young; perhaps the lad would prove to be without talent for the job of feudal lord… Such worries came crowding in on him.

It was then that his eye lit on this particular young son of his, who in infancy gave the impression of being a stoutly-built, bright and physically imposing lad. He was provided with what today would be termed an education for the gifted, but it was quickly realised that while the rest of him might be impressive, this apparently did not extend to the contents of his brain.

'Might I venture to observe, your lordship,' a senior vassal remarked, 'that he is entirely different from yourself at that age.'

His lordship observed the boy, and understood that the first problem was his attitude. He couldn't remain formally seated on the floor for any length of time, but very soon began to stretch out his legs, turn and stare out the window, and set about picking his nose, which he did so excessively that he developed nosebleeds, ending up in the care of the castle physician.

His lordship grimaced to witness this, and rashly remarked, 'True enough, he's a different kettle of fish from me. Can he really have sprung from my loins?' – thus infuriating his wife.

Apart from the main castle, the domain also had a smaller West Castle, a secondary castle the very existence of which, in these days when regulations stipulated one castle per domain, was owing to the trust that the Shogun had placed in his lordship. Here his lordship's wife huffily announced that she was taking their son. His lordship opposed the idea, of course, but his wife was the esteemed daughter of a certain important feudal lord, and if word got out that there was a falling out between them the consequences would be worse still.

In fact, his lordship held a further grudge against his son. He himself had been small from birth and loathed the compulsory practice of martial arts; it had been decided that in combat with his trainer the opponent would always obligingly arrange to lose. But an appraising look at his son told him that for his age the boy was sturdy, robust and tall. What was more, he was popular with those around him, unlike that other spotty little boy had been.

Empty-headed though he was, he was a mild and amiable child whom others were drawn to pamper. 'Beware of one's juniors,' says Confucius (implying that their capacities are easily underestimated) and this seemed a fine instance of the aphorism. His own cravenness, so unbecoming in a 'great lord', filled him with disgust.

Such a state of mind will quickly communicate itself, and the lad was reserved with him; his lordship felt awkward if left alone with him, mere child though he was. This being the case, he had seized this opportunity to dispatch his son to the West Castle with a vast mountain of books and the injunction to read them all, along with special tutors to enforce the order, and heaved a private sigh of relief.

Back now to our freshly awakened young lordship. What happened next? A group of ladies-in-waiting first flocked to his side to briskly wash his face and dress him, then two identical trays were prepared for breakfast, and he sat motionless and still half-asleep, waiting until the pre-tasting was completed in another room and the food was declared free of poison.

'Why does that man eat by himself first?' he would ask innocently, his bewildered air causing great merriment. In fact, the same ritual had been conducted in the main castle, and since it happened every day he knew the answer perfectly well, but this was all that it occurred to him to say. The ladies-in-waiting took it in turns to laugh obligingly.

Once the whirlwind of early morning procedures was over, his natural childish impulse was to run about in the spacious room, but there was no indulging this for his tutors were already awaiting him, eager to train him up to match his father as quickly as possible. Preparations for the role of lord of the castle; rules of etiquette; readings from the works of the great sages of the past; practice of the special signature to append to documents, just a little different from that of his father; the composition of written directives; letter-writing; copying of Chinese texts – all manner of learning assailed him.

He struggled to resist with a combination of moans, shrieks and tears, and cries of 'What's this? What's it for?', but 'Nursey', the name for his old wet nurse (his real mother had recently died), knew his game.

'Come now, your lordship, what do you mean! At your age your father could compose poems in Japanese and Chinese! You must keep to the contract and be prepared to follow in his footsteps someday soon…' Her fingers rapped the tatami matting on which she sat, or drew lines and circles to reinforce her point, while her unnervingly steely gaze remained fixed on him.

'Okay okay! And what's with this "someday soon"? Stuffing my head full of too many facts is just like stuffing my stomach with too much food!'

Today you'd probably call it adolescent rebellion. Nothing anyone said could please him.

It's true that back in the old days of warfare a boy of his status could live in hope of the prize of taking some enemy general's head, or could leap to sudden prominence with a moment's lucky chance to reveal his military prowess. But those days were over. Instead, his daily or monthly accomplishments were judged on how quickly he got through the books his father had set him. It was well known that all this talk of catching up with his father 'someday soon' was just empty morale-boosting.

Thanks to Nursey's constant repetition of the phrase, he began to be secretly referred to by the nickname Lord Asunaro, or Lord Someday-soon, both within the castle and beyond its walls. The name is a play on words. *Asunaro* is actually the name of a kind of conifer, a little-known tree that is similar to the more well-known hinoki, the Japanese cedar so greatly prized for its appearance and its use as a building material. The sound of the word, and how it is written, however, also suggests a meaning along the lines of 'to become something someday soon'. Legend even has it that the *asunaro* tree yearned that tomorrow it would be a hinoki. In fact, those are the two characters used to write its name. Why the fetching and fast-growing *asunaro* tree should aspire to become a gloomy cedar 'someday soon' is anyone's guess. As with the vegetable known as *ashitaba* (literally 'tomorrow's leaf', a variety of angelica), the name usually carries overtones of pristine freshness and of superior quality. It was, however, not for any such fine attributes that our young lord acquired his mocking nickname; but Nursey's constant admonitions to our unfortunate young lord caused his nickname to stick.

The young Lord Asunaro lived in a protected inner part of the castle where limited sunlight penetrated, owing to the way the walls and pillars met to form a kind of spiral.

The death of a feudal ruler was always extremely problematic, both publicly and privately, which is why this ruler-to-be spent his days thus protected, and quite unoccupied apart from his tedious studies. The main castle maintained a strict division between the inner area and the retainers' quarters, to prevent the possibility of anything untoward occurring between them and the ladies in the lord's service. The West Castle was much the same, enclosed by a protective moat, which in turn was surrounded by the homes of senior retainers, beyond which were the houses of the samurai class, distantly ringed by a wide area of townsfolk's dwellings. In other words, the whole place was arranged in a great protective coil that prevented the direct approach of any enemy.

Now that all this caution had become unnecessary with the new era of peace, the work of the retainers had radically altered. One by one the men who strutted their stuff in the retainers' quarters, squaring their shoulders and striking their muscled arms and proudly proclaiming their feats in gruff voices – 'Back then I used to take 'em on three at a time, you know!' and so on – were slowly disappearing.

As for the castle watchtowers, they no longer fulfilled any function beyond an empty display of power. The new era's first 'Supreme Ruler', the great and immensely popular Lord Nobunaga Oda (1534-1582), was probably the only person to actually inhabit his watchtower – he seems to have lived on the very top floor of the castle tower at Azuchi (a castle he himself had had built). This we can surmise from the fact that it was quite unlike the usual bare and uncouth watchtowers found elsewhere. The splendour of this watchtower room, replete with splendid screen paintings and covered in magnificent red lacquer, seems to suggest that he himself lived there. It must have been no easy matter to be in the irascible Nobunaga's service, climbing up and down these steep narrow stairs in the days before elevators and escalators in order to see to his needs.

Nobunaga was the last of the great warlords of an earlier era, when warfare was rife and watchtowers were an essential part of any castle. The climate played a role in this story; from the late 16th to the early 17th centuries, the earth underwent a sudden temporary cooling. Crops failed and the people grew troubled, and Japan entered the so-called 'Warring States' period, when men fought each other for local power. In Europe there were similar upheavals, with the loss of faith in the Church leading to terrible religious wars.

This chaotic time ended in the early 17th century, when the climate stabilised and in Japan food became less scarce again, and people grew tired of the continual warfare and at last embraced peace. This was mirrored in Europe with, for instance, the establishment of Bourbon rule in France, whose monarchs united

France as the Shoguns did Japan, and the subsequent Golden Age. In other words, this had been a moment when the earth chose to assert itself a little and remind everyone that it is a living being.

Despite the onset of a peaceful age in Japan, the old medieval status system nevertheless continued into the new era in much the same way as the castle watchtowers remained long after they had ceased to have any real function. The hereditary lines of senior retainers still maintained their status even when the sons were incompetent; but for most of the ordinary samurai, literary and calligraphic skills were now deemed of greater worth than military prowess, and the abacus had become a crucial tool in their arsenal.

Each autumn there was an 'arithmetical competition' among the youthful retainers. It was really more a sort of employment exam than the equivalent of our university entrance tests, and the young were trained up for it in the art of Japanese mathematics at a version of the modern-day cram school. Competition was fierce, but the winners were permitted to attend the Accounting Bureau to learn the trade. Thus a group of young accountants gathered on the castle's ground floor, and the click of abacus beads and the rustle of turning pages pervaded the place like the murmur of flowing water. Morning, noon and evening a large drum was sounded, signifying nothing more barbarous than the orderly passage of time.

Within this murmurous flow of sound was a flurry and bustle of special allowances, stipend amounts, pay reductions, loans, reimbursements and much else. Some might have been expected to complain that, with all this, surely anachronistic expenses such as the watchtower and suchlike, maintained solely for appearances' sake, should be discontinued – but the mere rumour of such a suggestion would have been enough to bring down a severe rebuke from on high. No matter how profligate the two castles were, it was nothing out of the ordinary; they must be maintained in style for appearance's sake.

Those ladies-in-waiting who swarmed around the young Lord Asunaro to dress him were likewise simply there for show. They supervised his every move, and they in turn were strictly overseen by old Nursey. All this may seem rather pointless, but it wasn't entirely so.

One day, when naughtiness had prompted Lord Asunaro to slip past the surrounding supervision, he suddenly heard bewitching voices coming from the shelter of the castle wall. It so happened that it was the third day of the third month, the day of the Peach Festival, and a group of young girls had gathered there to play.

Toddling over, he discovered a scene quite unlike that of the courtyard garden with its round eave tiles that met his grim gaze every morning – a room replete with vases of peach blossom. And there, before his very eyes for the first time, were young girls his own age, some among them already tall enough to be wearing adult-length kimonos. Both in scent and in deportment they were quite unlike the ladies-in-waiting who normally crowded around him.

'Oh, there's some young man here!' cried a voice, and instantly – oh calamity! – he was surrounded, and with cries of 'Gracious, how do you come to be dressed like this?' was seized by the sleeves, collar and hem and dragged along by them all, and before he could say a word Lord Asunaro found himself tumbled onto the tatami matting.

Children used to play various games back then – alphabet cards, *sugoroku*, top-spinning, battledore and shuttlecock, hide-and-seek, playing houses and doll play – and until that moment a festive game of dolls had been in progress, but it was quite forgotten with the advent of the young lord.

There were gentle questions: 'So where are you from? Do tell us your name.'

'Er... I'm the young lord.' He had intended it to sound dignified, but he found himself reeling at the startling new fragrance he breathed, and his voice trembled.

'He must have strayed here somehow.'

'It's a special festival today. Do come and play with us for a while.'

The sweet sake that was set before the festival doll display was poured into a red lacquered cup for him. The fumes of the finely brewed malted rice liquor were strong enough to choke on.

'It will go to your head if you drink it down all at once! Slowly, slowly, yes, that's right...'

Handled like a child yet so sweetly and tenderly, the young Lord Asunaro was enveloped in the scent of their incense-permeated robes.

'Oh you drank that *so* well! Just like a true lord.'

He stood there simply agog, his shoulders slumped.

'Listen, here's a delightful game we can play. Now that you're tipsy, you can be *It* for hide-and-seek.'

In no time he found his eyes bound with a silk cloth.

'... Here, over here! Where my hands are clapping!' But although the voices rose all around him, the sake seemed to have gone to his head and he could only stagger about on unsteady feet. Following the sounds of cajoling cries, laughter, shrieks and the rustle of clothing he made a guess and leapt, managing to grab someone and bring her down, and as they tumbled his hand slipped into her sleeve and down, meeting velvety flesh there; his weight came down on top of her, and from beneath him he heard a tantalising little squeal.

How long did it last? The ladies-in-waiting came upon him as he lay unresistingly sprawled there, quickly followed by old Nursey clutching the inevitable memorandum book to her breast, who proceeded to berate the girls.

'Why pick on them?' he objected crossly. 'Surely I'm the one in the wrong for running away and coming here!' But his head was filled only with the memory of that enticing little squeal.

'Good gracious, young sir, just look at you!' She grimly surveyed his rumpled clothing. 'If his lordship were to see you now there'd be worse than hell to pay!'

At that age – although some of those girls were in fact rather mature for their age – nothing very momentous could have occurred, and they got off with no more than a scolding. But from this day onwards, something in Lord Asunaro collapsed and something new began to germinate in its stead. A suspicion gripped him that in this world (by which he meant the castle) there was some unfathomable thing, as utterly different from the ordinary as heaven is from earth, and henceforth his days, until now so absolutely predictable, went askew.

The impressive significance of the corner tower, which Nursey had explained as being 'built by your father in case anything happens, with the aim of keeping your lordship safe and sound', now began to fade from his mind. What seethed and flickered constantly in its place was the sensation of that girl's breast against his hand down her sleeve, and that little squeal that she uttered when his weight came down on top of her. (What sort of cry was that, for heaven's sake?)

'You must show your mettle as your father's heir, and dedicate yourself single-mindedly to your tasks...'

It was Nursey's familiar harsh voice.

'Well, father might be wonderful, but surely all I'm doing is just imitation. Don't you think so, Nursey?'

This was only the second time in her long service that he had argued back like this, and it flustered her. 'Now it's not as simple as that, you know. You have to get past this stage, that's the thing. Constant vigilance, firm tenacity...'

'So when is that corner tower going to get used?'

'Well, it's symbolic. The day it actually came in useful would be a very frightening day...'

'See? That's what I mean!'

Staring up at the coffered ceiling, Lord Asunaro picked his nose and considered. While there was no way to understand what had gone on that day with the girls, it was certainly something quite different from any game he'd played before. Usually, it was a matter of tussles with the retainers' young sons. Be it wrestling or hand-to-hand combat, even when his opponent was a big fellow it turned out before he knew it that he'd won. Of course that's the way things had been fixed, and sure enough he had realised this and was bored mindless by it. As for his other tough training, of that more later.

Thenceforth, our young lord took to giving the slip to his nurse and ladies-in-waiting and creeping off to the girls' quarters to play. For it was, after all, another realm, one that not only dazzled the eye but delighted both the nose and the hands.

At this time, the most expensive item in the governance of the domain was not anything to do with externalities but rather its innermost area: those ladies' quarters into which the young Lord Asunaro now stole. He was no longer either surprised or perturbed these days by the welcome he received there – the way the girls clung to him and seized him by whatever part of his clothing they fancied, in much the same fashion as women of the street soliciting for custom. So far, though, whichever girl he pulled to the floor and lay on (and truth to tell he couldn't really tell who was who) would only give that little squeal, and that was all that ever happened in this game.

Lord Asunaro's
New Realm

One day, however, he saw standing before him an elegant, beautiful and unknown maiden, impressively attired. She would have been a little older than him, but there was no hint of condescension as, with a soft smile, she made him a little bow.

Astonishment manifested itself in a small moan that broke from his lips. He stood there rooted to the spot, gazing up at her. Small though his brain might be, his height was considerable – one reason he had been chosen as successor – but now he suddenly found his eyes trained upward.

'Here, miss, come and play with us! Come on!' came the encouraging cries from around her, but the maiden lingered on there, apparently lost to the world, and the young Lord Asunaro, quite deprived of words, was impelled forward and reached to seize her sleeve.

She dodged him nimbly, hair ornaments tinkling, and gave a laugh.

'I've been hearing a lot of rumours about your lordship and now I come to see you, you do look delightful fun.' Her aplomb, so different from the other girls with their little squeals, was bracingly cool.

Ignoring the pestering cries urging him to be quick and take her hand, Lord Asunaro instead followed her beckoning hand and walked to a corner of the main hall. There his unobservant eyes discovered for the first time a low folding screen decorated with paintings in the elegant Tosa School Japanese style, which sheltered a stepped display stand, a little mother-of-pearl writing desk, and on it a gold inlay inkstone case and other writing implements.

The maiden settled herself before the desk with a toss of her skirts that threw out a waft of scent, drew a piece of paper from the lacquered letter box, and swiftly wrote a poem:

> Much though this promises delight
> > alas I must away
> > > to the maternal waiting arms

This she handed to him, and as he took it and raised it to his forehead in dazed thanks, with a rustle of clothing and a little smile, delicious to the eye and ear, she vanished beyond the sliding doors.

Just as he had failed to notice that the aforementioned items of furniture had arrived on special
order from the capital and were outrageously extrava-
gant, in the same way he could unfortunately make no
sense of the elegant poem she had given him.

Observing this later, Nursey felt compelled to speak.
'That was Lady Unokimi, you know. Well well, it's still
an unformed hand, but this is impressively graceful
writing. So what have you done for a response poem?'

'What? … A response poem? … I've no idea… Er,
she's going home to her mother, right? I could say I'm
envious… Um…'

Here he ground to a halt. Nursey had good reason
to cast him a pitying look, for his own mother had died
not long after the move to the West Castle.

'Where does she come from anyway?' he demanded,
suddenly fierce.

'Well, this must go no further than your ears, but
actually she's someone who his lordship took in owing
to a certain family situation. But all that has resolved
itself and now she's to return to her mother's place.
That's probably why she chose to show herself like that
and gave you the parting gift of a poem. It's just such
a shame that you haven't sent her any poem in reply…'

"Ha… What's a silly old response poem?' He
gave a loud sniff and pretended to shrug the whole

thing off, yet deep within him stirred a feeling of enchantment that was later to undergo a truly great transformation...

People today don't care for the thought of anyone past early youth relying on the help of a group of ladies to see to the little day-to-day details of their life. But since infancy Lord Asunaro had never been in a position to compare himself with others, so it didn't strike him as at all odd. It was likewise simply part of the routine for the ritual of food-tasting to be performed before meals twice a day, since the survival of the lord was crucial.

One day he belatedly brought up the subject again. 'I hear the food-tasting still goes on. Is that true?'

'Your food is tasted without fail in the next room before it is brought to you.'

'I see. Well if he's going to all this trouble, let's have it done here in front of my eyes.'

'Dear me no, such an unpleasant sight...'

'I'll be the one to decide that. Quick, have him eat it right here.'

The designated official hastily placed the tray in front of his lordship, but the tension was extreme.

'Come come, relax while you eat. Aha, so that's where you put the chopsticks, eh? People are really all the same, aren't they? I see, you do make a lot of noise when you chew. I wonder why.' He was craning forward to watch, intent on missing nothing.

'My most humble apologies. I was unaware that I would offend your ears, your lordship…'

'Yes, I see. You have a big fleshy jaw, that may be why there's all this noise. Well well, I never knew it was so interesting to watch someone eating. What dish will you go to next? The right one? The left one?'

In increasing confusion, and anxious to be done as soon as possible, the young samurai accidentally tipped over the soup bowl.

'Oops, over it goes! I sometimes do that too. But there's a bit of rice stuck to your cheek, you know. Well that was excellent, I'm impressed with the way you eat, the way you chew, and your terrific speed.'

It should be pointed out that throughout the feudal period, the status system was as complex as a spider's web. Those who personally served the lord were of the highest distinction, but this was not necessarily accompanied by a rise in their allotted stipend. In terms of salary, food-tasters were on a very different rung from those of good birth and lineage, so one had to accept that they bolted their food. For your average samurai the aim was to get it into you quickly, and out the other end with similar speed.

'Fancy that. I never knew there was such a fine spectacle. So my retainers have all been hiding this from me, *ha ha ha*!'

Leaning over the elbow rest before him, his neck extended like a tortoise, Lord Asunaro was in great good humour from start to finish.

Hearing of this 'outrage', Nursey appeared clutching her memorandum book to her breast. 'What's all this, your lordship! That young fellow is in such a state that he's taken to his bed and others have had to take over his duties. You mustn't go making fun of people like that!'

'Eh? You mean he's upset over that? Oh dear, I'm sorry, I didn't mean to do anything bad.'

Nursey's face tightened. 'You must realise there can be situations where the effect is the same, no matter what your intentions.'

Suddenly Lord Asunaro struck the elbow rest a violent blow. 'What? What are you saying? It's nothing to do with me! I haven't got a thing to do all day. If that fellow's upset, well, fine by me. He did as ordered and I praised him, that's all I can do.'

'But that's just it, surely your efforts must be devoted wholeheartedly to improving yourself so that someday soon…'

'…!'

'I recall personally hearing you announce that you were going to do your best to master the art of poetry,' Nursey continued reprovingly.

'That's quite true. And thanks to that what happened? A fresh mountain of books has landed on me!' he spat. 'Behind them is that other mountain of books my father sent me. What fun, eh?' And he gave her a bold grin.

When the morning drum sounded, it marked the start of a lecture by the Confucian scholar Tagonoura Kainosuke. The tale of the episode with the food-taster had spread throughout the domain, and beyond the castle walls Lord Asunaro's next mad antics – as they were called in the castle – were apparently anticipated with much delight.

Reverently, Tagonoura opened the Confucian *Analects*. His plan seemed to have been to proceed through the Four Classics – *The Great Learning, The Doctrine of the Mean, The Analects* and *The Sayings of Mencius* – but the young lord had sat there half asleep throughout, barely listening. For this reason, the scholar had changed the order, and turned to *The Analects* as something with which the young lord would have at least a passing familiarity.

'Confucius determined the progression of life according to a man's years, but in fact things don't work out that way. I myself, for instance, am in my sixties…'

'"*In one's sixties one's ears follow*", isn't it?' As always, the young lord had the elbow rest before him and was leaning on it, his chin resting on folded arms.

'That's right, well done. "*In one's forties one has no doubts, in one's fifties one knows the will of heaven, in one's sixties one's ears follow*", Confucius says. In other words, all knowledge flows naturally and one clearly understands what others say…'

The young lord suddenly thrust out a hand.

'There's something I want to say to you in private. No one else must get wind of it, so come in a little closer. What, feeling shaky are you? Painful legs? Well then, I'll move over there.'

'No, with all due respect your lordship—'

But Lord Asunaro had brought his mouth close to the panicking Tagonoura's cheek, and suddenly he bit his ear.

'How… outrageous!'

Lord Asunaro bared his bloodied teeth in a grin as he watched Tagonoura writhe on the floor.

'I thought if your ears aren't surprised by things any more that might mean they're half dead, but actually your ear had quite a crunch to it, considering. Now give me your other ear,' and he leaned forward to seize it, whereupon the scholar scrambled away on all fours, clutching his bloodied ear.

'Not so fast. I still have something to say.'

'Wh…what is that?'

'That ear of yours. Having sampled it I must say, it's not something worth following, *ha ha ha*.'

A number of different lecturers came in turns, but on the next occasion it was a young man who appeared in Tagonoura's stead.

'Er… my father is still receiving treatment, so I've come in his place. I'm Hironoshin, your lordship.'

At this, the young Lord Asunaro grinned. Sure enough, like father like son – Hironoshin's ears stuck out just like his father's. 'According to the castle doctor Chugensai it was a remarkably deep wound,' the young lord remarked. 'He was most impressed. Well it goes to show my teeth are sharp, anyway. They did quite a bit of damage it seems. So how is he now?'

'Well it's more the emotional distress that is confining him to his bed, your lordship,' the young man replied diffidently.

'I'm not exactly crazy you know. He was being ridiculous, carrying on about passing on the sayings of the sages by word of mouth and so on, so I thought "Okay, let's try that for real" and I put my face up close, and I just had this sudden impulse to bite his ear. Now I'd like to pass something on to you by word of mouth too. Come over here a bit closer.' Lord Asunaro bared his teeth and his nostrils flared.

'Heaven forbid! Spare me please!' Hironoshin was edging backwards.

'Hmm. No point in comparing the taste of your ear I suppose. So tell me, if you have to do with the words of the sages, you must become quite unworldly, no?'

'Well not exactly…'

'Can you ever become like your father do you think? Maybe not today, but someday soon?'

'No, I'm sure I couldn't.'

'When the young lady brought the tea just now you glanced at her. Were you checking how pretty or ugly she is?'

'Good heavens no…'

'What a boring mind you have. Okay, even if you didn't see her face you'd remember what she was wearing, no?'

'Oh no, I know nothing of such things, you see…'

'It was dyed to match the colours of autumn. Didn't you notice?'

'That is my inadequacy.'

'Hmm. The blocked ears of a saint? I won't eat you. There is no need to tremble.'

After that Hironoshin collapsed with stress and these lectures came to an end. The ear-biting started rumours and gossip. But nobody actually criticised the young lord. This was because the father and son scholars, sent by the lord, had become even more arrogant than previously, generating huge animosity.

Young though Lord Asunaro was, this was by any standards willful behaviour. But his father chose to prevaricate rather than interrogate him on the matter, and for this there was a precedent.

The boy's instructions in swordsmanship had begun back when he was eleven and still living in the main castle. The lord himself was not fond of swordsmanship, which perhaps was behind his choosing to assign the now-retired Satomi Eizan as instructor. Apparently stirred by this, Satomi Eizan grew boastful about a youth spent practicing his skills throughout the land, and was inclined to deal with the lad in a rather offhand manner.

'Okay then, try this,' announced Lord Asunaro one day, handing him a pickled white radish while he himself took up the wooden sword. (The protective gear and light bamboo swords of today's swordsmanship practice were yet to be invented, and only appeared and gained wide acceptance at the end of the feudal period.)

'This? Very well, very good,' said Satomi Eizan, gripping the white radish and planting himself in combat stance. 'One such as yourself is hardly likely to get the better of me, after all.'

But the words had barely left his mouth when the wooden sword came down on him, and as he twisted to dodge it his legs were swept from under him, followed by first one blow then another to his instinctively huddled shoulders.

'Oh you don't strike the legs, your lordship!' people cried as they rushed in to stop him.

'Just think yourselves lucky I stopped him at the legs and not on his pate,' declared Lord Asunaro, tossing the sword away. 'Surely the reason they wear armour and leg guards in battle is precisely because there's no such thing as rules there.'

For some reason this brazen nonchalance went largely unrebuked by his father.

Nevertheless, years later now, there was no hiding the impression that the young lord's brain was still not as well developed as his physique.

'It's all very well to have yourself spoken of in these terms.' Clutching her memorandum book as she spoke, Nursey's troubled voice grew fruity. 'But you must understand that it does not improve your progress towards attaining the lordship someday soon if you go on cancelling lesson after lesson like this.'

'Huh. What earthly use are those things anyway? Are you trying to tell me that I'll get to Daddy's position in life just by reading and hearing stuff? Don't be ridiculous.'

Over near the wall lay a scattering of the books he had read, with beyond them the inexorable towering cliffs of those as yet unread, a bulk that never changed. Witnessing now how astonishingly fragile that vast boulder that stood on his steep path to his father's position had turned out to be, how easily that brittle rock had crumbled in the face of those little explosions of his, something deep inside him melted utterly away, leaving behind it only a gaping chasm.

'Now then, your lordship, what do you plan to do about your study of poetry? If you don't care for it, will you give it up?' Nursey asked, pressing home the issue.

He had made light of the idea with the claim that it was much easier than the usual strings of Chinese characters he had to plough through in his studies, but he reeled at the number of musty tomes of poetics that had arrived as a result of his announcement. His brain was required to negotiate the complexities of poetic association, adaptations of famous poems, poetic puns, poetic epithets, the background to the names of the poets, and more besides, with the dexterity of an intellectual ninja.

He must also be thoroughly inculcated in the art of writing in the mixed Japanese and Chinese script style. There were collections of model handwriting from the past to be studied as well, and short excerpts of handwriting deemed particularly superior. The calligraphic skill of the nobility, monks, poets and military men of the period is quite astonishing, but as with the European quill pen calligraphy of earlier times, necessity made it in fact a natural accomplishment. Samurai of the lower classes would spend what little money they had to provide their children with writing implements. As the only career paths open to them were gained through learning and calligraphic skills, their expensive brushes never stopped even when their equally expensive paper was as good as reduced to fibres with the wear and tear of the black mass of repeated brushstrokes. 'Home schooling', in which the brushstrokes were practiced with a stick in smoothed sand or earth, was entirely normal.

The first books to make an appearance in this education were always the twenty-one imperial poetry anthologies that provided the poetic models. He would have been happy to regain his former lazy existence, but Lord Asunaro soon found himself forced like a plant in a hothouse by two tutors who hovered constantly behind him like a pair of puppeteers, nagging endlessly over posture, thickness or thinness of ink, the various ways to finish the brushstrokes, and the rest.

Now, however, his reaction was different from the days of those torments of Chinese writing practice. Years later though it now was, his bitter regret at having failed to send Lady Unokimi a response poem that day was still fresh. The image of that maiden – so different from the other girls with their little squeals – who had written the beautiful poem with its beautiful brushstrokes and then disappeared along with her tinkling hair ornaments and her scent, only grew more vivid in his memory with the passage of time.

Afterwards, he had pulled the story together from various fragments of information. Politics had apparently lain behind her presence there, essentially as a kind of hostage, and that elegant behaviour of hers had quite likely derived from a keen awareness that, all things being equal, she was destined to become his wife.

This discovery not only moved him deeply in ways he had hitherto never experienced, but he also felt physically flooded with an urgent energy that welled up from within. Wiping away a bitter tear, he had understood that some mere response poem would hardly have begun to answer this situation, but all this he kept strictly to himself.

'From what I can see, you are throwing yourself into the art of poetry as you've never done with anything before,' declared Nursey, with a bow so low that the memorandum book she clutched to her breast was in danger of folding double. 'I am deeply gratified, your lordship!'

When Lord Asunaro learned that there was plan afoot for Lady Unokimi to make a strategic marriage – something so taken for granted in this period that no one remarked on it – and that she would now move even further away, he bit his upper lip and tearfully composed the following poem:

> To and fro the tide doth shift –
> but when it's at the full
>   cross to me o'er these castle walls

…although in fact Nursey and the tutors had, with all due respect for his lordship, had a significant hand in its composition. This was sent without further ado to Lady Unokimi, and presently a response arrived.

> The deeps remain unknown, and yet
> however high the wave
>   this far *tide* cannot cross back to you

At a cursory reading, those opening words 'the deeps remain unknown' could be taken to mean that, regardless of the intentions of others, within her own hidden depths… Nevertheless, there was no getting around the fact that in a nutshell (or even out of one for that matter) that expression 'the far *tide*', whose words clearly contained a pun on 'to be "tied" in wedlock', meant she would not be coming back.

This precipitated the fall, with a resounding crash, of the final great stone of that crumbling edifice within Lord Asunaro's heart. His 'penchant' for the girls, which had already begun to raise a few eyebrows around him, now set in in earnest. It had all the appearances of a lascivious abandonment to desire. But in those days there was no thought of discreetly rearranging things to keep such activities out of view; one simply chose not to see what went on among one's superiors. The feudal ban on all unrest meant that peace and harmony were prized in all situations.

Such a 'penchant' of a designated lord must soon become pertinent to the question of succession. In point of fact, our young lord had by now taken as his wife the daughter of a certain minor lord. In the first few years he had to contend with the oversight of his father, and as heir he was required to devote himself to producing a further heir. His dedication to the task produced four daughters. But, as you will be aware, a daughter cannot become a feudal lord, and so his interest in his wife finally flagged, and his attentions were diverted to, of all things, her ladies-in-waiting. The result of this licentiousness was that his relations with his wife had long since become, to use a modern term, a matter of going through the motions.

Once this had begun, it was as though the lid was taken off. His 'penchant' extended to those girls he used to play with, one and all, but now their behaviour was a far cry from that almost nostalgic little squeal they used to give – instead, they now clung to him. He still had no real idea who was who.

And now it was that that same Nursey of old reappeared, almost as if she had been awaiting her moment in the wings, and set about gliding from room to room, memorandum book and writing brush in hand. Lord though he was, he could not indulge his 'penchant' quite as he pleased. A diligent record must be kept of every occasion, time and date on which Lord Asunaro took a certain woman to bed, and when Nursey met him next she would cover her face with the memorandum book and form a circle with thumb and forefinger as a silent sign of acknowledgement, while for some reason emitting a toadlike croak.

It is not difficult to understand the crucial importance of this role of hers. For one thing, it was necessary to establish that these acts of his were committed by himself and not somebody else. For another, a son born of a certain coupling does not necessarily turn out to accurately reflect the status of the partner. It may well be that someone of good lineage might give birth to a complete fool, or some lowly person produce a quite outstanding child. Lord Asunaro might be able to 'pass' thanks to his father, but if a feudal master was too feebleminded everyone from his retainers to the farmers would be merciless, and at worst it could even lead to the dissolution of the domain itself.

This important department, euphemistically referred to as 'the women's rooms', was of no more practical use than the outmoded watchtower in this time of peace, and like the tower bore no relationship to the actual business of running the domain. Yet insofar as it was what you might call an experimental nursery for the next generation, its relationship to the entire domain was quietly pervasive.

Naturally, the lord's abandonment morning, noon and night to the indulgences that free time and his matchless sexual appetite prompted with all and sundry was disparaged and condemned both privately and publicly. But the fact is that the women were engaged in a desperate struggle to bear him a child outstanding both physically and mentally, and were it not for this the following situation could not have arisen.

Tomorrow Comes:
Lord Asunaro's Ascent

At length Lord Asunaro's father announced his retirement and, perhaps due to his rage at the news of his son's antics, very soon afterwards died, leaving our young lord to succeed both in name and in actuality as heir. In truth he should now return to the main castle, but his father's aura hung heavy in the air there, and the old guard who had favoured his father were still in place. For this reason Lord Asunaro remained at the West Castle, so let us continue to call him 'the young lord'.

With the passage of time, this young lord's inclination for the practice of poetry and literature intensified.

Actually, in this peaceful age all feudal lords to varying degrees replaced their now largely useless military skills with a lurch towards the cultural tastes of the aristocracy. Centuries earlier, back in the late Heian period of the 12th century, it was understood by all concerned that the armed retainers who protected the emperor and aristocracy were termed samurai, while the more lowly general military arms bearers went by the name of *mononofu*. There was little to distinguish these two, in fact, both being essentially groups of sanctioned murderers. In any other country, it would unsurprising if the emperor and his aristocrats, incapable as they were of gripping anything but chopsticks or a writing brush, were sooner or later exterminated and the nation seized; the fact that this didn't happen in Japan was because, as we have seen with our young lord, despite their military power these people felt a deep admiration for the cultured aristocratic world of the capital, and a yearning to imitate its elegant ways.

Having sweated so hard over his response poem, it was natural that this should then become the breakthrough that set Lord Asunaro yearning to import the entire world of the capital lock, stock and barrel into his provincial world.

Designed as it was for warfare, the West Castle was a bleak and gloomy place without an ounce of cultured elegance. The so-called inner section was termed The Long Room – a large area in the middle of the long narrow building that was divided into a series of small apartments of equal size. The partitions were so thin that everything could be heard through them, in effect rather like a modern piggery or a cheap lodging house. Each small apartment consisted of a room of six tatami mats plus another half the size, and a cooking area. Essentially a version of the old Heian period architecture, with its large spaces divided into smaller ones by temporary partitions, there was no way to renovate beyond spending money on interior decoration with the aim of introducing court chic.

Lord Asunaro first set about hanging fine reed screens with scarlet cloth borders, in imitation of palace furnishings. He set up a statue of the Buddha ornamented with metal foil (a far cry from his father's hostility to Buddhism), and bought in whatever money could purchase in the way of gold folding screens, long-handled silk parasols, multi-layered formal ladies' gowns in the old style, traditional coiffures, hair ornaments, fans and so forth. He delighted in playing the old court football, dressed in courtier's clothing, and indulging in the best Fushimi sake and side dishes. This was all very well, but there was something pathetic about these phoney pretentions.

Not only local girls but real live 'ladies of the capital' were imported from Kyoto, the old capital where the emperor still resided, to play the role of palace ladies-in-waiting, with names such as Wakana, Fujitsubo and Ukifune, taken straight from the heroines of the famous *The Tale of Genji*. He and his ladies of the capital conversed with each other in the refined old Kyoto language and composed charming poems together, and he yearned to somehow replicate the courtly Winding Waters Banquet, in which elegant ladies floated poems down a little winding stream. Days and nights spent tipping sake from flask into a lacquered cup and thence into his mouth, however, eventually led to even our paragon of potency lying sprawled dead drunk upon the floor.

For their own part, these ladies of the capital, acquired through the kind offices of a court noble and at unstinting expense, were happy enough to live there in luxury. It was a great improvement on their poverty-stricken existences back in Kyoto, even though they found provincial feudal lords far from attractive. In effect, these lasses had come with the full consciousness that they were essentially hand-me-downs from the capital and must relinquish all pride.

Naturally enough, it would be foolish to assume that just because they came from the capital they could all compose poetry, or be relied on always to provide witty conversation. But the local girls, brought up as they were among the mountains, no matter how pleasing to the eye were consistently boring... Yet in fact, for all the rumours, our young lord brought into his bedroom even the lowly kitchen maid who served the smug ladies of the capital, so what can one say?

Seeing how devoted were the feudal lords to indolence and dissipation, we today might imagine that they were heading for an early death from lifestyle-related disease due to nutritional over-indulgence. Actually, however, the food consumed by lords both at the time and later was far from luxurious; in fact, modern-day Japanese have the highest calorie intake in Japan's history, approaching that of European aristocrats of earlier times.

Moreover, there were greater physical demands. Feudal lords were required to spend a year, albeit every other year, in the governmental seat of power in Edo, setting out from their country domains in the spring on a journey to Edo lasting well over two weeks – probably not something that a grossly overweight man could withstand. Then there were the physical arts, which included the wrestling and hand-to-hand combat mentioned earlier, although both these involved certain constraints and hence Lord Asunaro found them rather tedious. There were no less than eighteen fundamental military arts to choose from, and the young lord was particularly fond of, and skilled at, archery and horsemanship (neither of which allowed for restraint). Indolent though he was, he was fit and robust.

Even back in the feudal era the main roads were well-maintained and policed, thanks to those lordly processions to and from Edo, while in Europe even into the 20th century brigands apparently infested the highways. Japan's 250 or so feudal lords travelled in state, sometimes with a large retinue. In due course the roads were further flooded by the immensely popular Ise pilgrimage known as Oise-mairi. Young and old, men and women – several million people a year took to the roads to visit the famous Ise Shrine. Hard though it is to believe, Edo folk even sent dogs off on this pilgrimage on their behalf. The dogs bore a special tag around their neck saying 'Proxy Pilgrim', and carried a bag containing funds for travelling expenses incurred. These dogs were helped on their way by people they encountered and apparently managed to travel the full 400 kilometres of the return journey from Edo, duly arriving home carrying the sacred Ise amulet for their master. Additionally, it is said that their travelling expenses weren't stolen, but increased. Such was the Edo period… but I digress.

Conveyed along in a splendid palanquin on their way to and from Edo, most feudal lords were unbearably bored – there was no way of opening a window to take in the comings and goings around you, and both retinue and bearers were single-mindedly intent on pushing on and getting through the journey as quickly as possible. When they arrived at one of the larger post stations the men could delight the crowds with the elaborate waving of the feathered spears that preceded the processions of feudal lords, but the lord himself could not witness any of this, and could only sit there in the cramped box clinging to the dangling rope handle provided and grimly attempt to withstand the constant lurchings of the palanquin. It was, in other words, an act of challenging austerity for the whole 600-strong procession.

Lord Asunaro's late father had whiled away the tedious days of these journeys with a selection of sizeable books from his library that he piled into the palanquin, leading his bearers to grumble behind his back at the impossible weight they had to lug, but the young lord was quite the opposite, and looked forward to the journeys with childlike delight. He noted down on a map everything of novelty, interest or fame that he would pass, and made a point of pausing to raise the blinds and investigate them. Declaring that Mount Fuji was marvellous, he would halt the procession on both inward and outward journeys at the same spot, and one and all they would gape at the mountain in slack-jawed amazement.

It was the practice when crossing paths with a feudal lord's procession to sink to one's knees at the roadside, and Lord Asunaro was likely to address a man who knelt before his palanquin thus:

'What say you? A fine view of the mountain again today, is it not? You must be delighted.'

'Indeed, begging your pardon, your lordship, it is a quite incomparable mountain, but we locals see it morning, noon and night so it's nothing special for us you see,' the unfortunate man might reply, desperate to be released from his discomfort as soon as possible.

'But, from what I hear, a single glance can extend one's life by days.'

'Well perhaps such a thing might once have... But actually, sir, there's bad weather on the mountain today.'

'Is that so now? Well well...' Lord Asunaro's gaze travelled from the foot to the summit of Mount Fuji, where a spring storm was swirling the snow, and his mouth gaped open again. And truly anyone seeing this mountain, whatever the weather, would find themselves gaping and forgetting to so much as blink.

If the night's lodgings happened to provide some old man who liked to talk, our young lord would ask to be regaled with tales strange and marvellous, and lean on his elbow rest, listening with deep delight, later writing them down in what was becoming a fat book.

Wherever you may travel, of course, you find professional ladies offering the horizontal pleasures, but naturally such things aren't always provided to order. Here is a poem he wrote that just happens to have survived, on the subject of being deprived of them:

Melancholy it is
to sleep alone
a moon afloat
upon the pillowing waves
on a wild rocky shore

Here too, as touched on further below, the poem reaches for metaphors of flowing seas and waves.

Once he arrived in Edo, though, he could really go to town. Pleasures enough to indulge in to his heart's delight were on offer at every turn, and he quickly forgot the tribulations of the journey. Back in those days, even upper echelon samurai would go out in disguise and frequent not only the red-light district but the various theatres as well. Some reached the point where they quite forgot to carry their swords on these excursions, resulting in a terrible dressing-down once they got back.

It was the norm for lords from all the provinces to maintain several residences of varying importance in Edo and other important cities, and one of the astonishingly modern aspects of this arrangement was the 'diplomatic immunity' enjoyed in these residences, which exempted them from the usual feudal bureaucratic intrusions. The main residence was, as it were, the public face of the domain, but even here our self-indulgent young lord would brazenly bring in his women and indulge virtually nightly in his 'penchant'.

One year, not long after this delightful season in the metropolis had drawn to a close and he had returned home to sigh over the boredom of provincial life again, word reached him that up in the north country Lady Unokimi had suddenly found herself widowed, and apparently planned, in her grief, to become a nun.

It was now or never! Seething with excitement, he gave it his best and produced the following poem to send her:

> Now as the season freezes
> > oh turn your boat's prow
> > > back to the warm currents of the past

Whether by sheer chance or following the natural progression of the imagery, flowing water again figures here. For a month or so he waited, heart racing with anticipation.

> Clinging to one now gone
> > I look about me –
> > > frost settles even on fall's sacred flowers

Even he could see that this implied not only a hardening of the will to take the Buddhist tonsure, but also perhaps the added meaning that her own hair was now frosted with white. Biting his upper lip in that habit of his, he valiantly suppressed his tears – and sure enough, almost obsessively, his usual activities began again with renewed vigour.

The underlying psychology of this suggests that it all started when his meeting with Lady Unokimi coincided with the recent death of his mother – who had dispensed neither hugs nor scoldings – so that the experience of first love had merged with the mother figure. It may be that if this meeting had progressed easily to marriage, all his subsequent outrageous behaviour would have been avoided.

According to a fine succinct translation of the historical records relating to this domain, Lord Asunaro was reputed to have had 70 children. The records that have come down to us list 21 sons and 31 daughters. With the addition of his heir, this gives a tally of 53; taking into account perhaps 16 or 17 who died in infancy and are therefore unrecorded, plus one or two adopted daughters, we have a total of around 70.

Or so it is written (see Afterword). This bizarrely meticulous totting up of numbers, with not only the careful inclusion of the one heir, but the calculation of survival rates (a reflection of our modern-day scepticism regarding the state of hygiene at that time), may have been aided by the records kept by Nursey, but it is nevertheless laughably typical of the pedantic Japanese mindset.

Brave warriors of the earlier Warring States period, intent on producing an outstanding heir, all had prolific numbers of offspring. In the later age of peace, the eleventh Shogun Ienari Tokugawa, a man in the mould of our Lord Asunaro in terms of virility, engendered 55 children; this is considered a record, but it falls considerably short of our young lord's tally. This was an age when barbarous acts against women were treated indulgently, but even so, there was no hiding these enormities of his, either within the domain or further afield.

It may be that, in this case, his father's invisible power as a Forebear ironically played a part. Such difficult relations with an overpowering predecessor have in fact been far from unusual in history. Think, for instance, of the interesting example of Louis XVI of France, who reigned at the height of Bourbon power but seemed to have been so intimidated by his illustrious forebears that he shrank from approaching princesses as potential partners and instead stayed in his room obsessively making omelettes, or so dark rumour had it – quite the opposite response to that of our young lord.

Anyway, so it was that at the West Castle it was an everyday event to see young Asunaro look-alikes of all ages at play, and women with bellies like watermelons waddling about – and, since warring factions naturally form when those who are similar proliferate, there would be much hurtling at considerable speed up and down corridors and through halls by children in clusters or in single file. Residents and neighbourhood folk referred to the place as 'The Watermelon Residence'.

Lord Asunaro kept a detached eye on all this while nonchalantly summoning actors to entertain him, holding musical parties, immersing himself in poetry composition with litterateurs, and cheerfully ignoring status distinctions to exchange convivial sake cups with his inferiors. An old record detailing the situation of the domains at this time castigates him for this, declaring that he should have modelled himself on previous generations, but it oddly refrains from severe criticism, let alone outright condemnation.

At length there were too many children for the castle to hold, and resort was made to distributing some among the retainers. This caused them huge problems, as they were landed not only with a child but with an accompanying supervisor as well. There is one instance, noted in a domain history that touches on the unhygienic conditions of the time, in which a child was handed over with the vague instruction to 'raise him in a relaxed fashion', only for him to die two years later.

A count was kept of the number of children, but of course there were the mothers to consider too. Childbirth was very risky for women, and there would certainly have been some who died in the process. Factoring in the unknown rate of pregnancies, it must have involved an incalculable amount of time and effort to produce 70 children. When you consider that beyond the women who successfully produced children there were no doubt many others – the one-night stands, the women who didn't become pregnant – it seems likely that he would have slept with well over 100 women.

Lord Asunaro's Legacy

Lord Asunaro lived unusually long for his times, dying at 76, and he left a farewell testament. The first line of this reads: 'A ruler must devote himself whole-heartedly to the domain's government, and refrain from indolence...' – but an uneasy conscience no doubt subsequently caused him to rewrite this as: 'Benevolence and compassion are of the utmost importance'. He also declared, 'No matter what the military art, one must not desire to excel...', which the above-mentioned domain history condemns as an unprecedented statement for someone from a military family.

In reality, of course, Lord Asunaro must not be underestimated, both for his fine calligraphy and writing and for bequeathing to posterity one of the nation's most outstanding gardens. Nevertheless the early tome, whose sole standard of judgement was the moral notion of integrity, concludes with the typically decisive statement that 'Fool though he was, his lack of wrongdoing was preferable to mere cunning wit'.

I have already mentioned that one of the under-lying causes of both Japan's Warring States period of upheaval and Europe's religious wars may well have been the global cooling that occurred at this time – indeed something similar was probably also behind the French Revolution. Right before it occurred Japan's notoriously dangerous volcano Mount Asama erupted, and around the same time there was also a great volcanic explosion in Iceland, where magma had become dangerously exposed. Clouds of volcanic ash covered the globe, once again crops failed, and Japan experienced the Great Tenmei Era Famine (1782-7), while in France a strange green rain fell, destroying grain and resulting in bread shortages. Marie Antoinette, the wife of the ruling monarch, is famously said to have proposed that if people had no bread 'let them eat cake' (this story is actually an early example of fake news). She and her husband Louis XVI, still superficially a couple, of course went on to meet their fates at the guillotine. In Japan the big Edo rice merchants, fearing the riots of the starving people, organised local centres to distribute emergency rations, thereby managing to avert any real threat to the governing powers.

Meurseult, the emotionally stunted protagonist of Albert Camus' novel *L'Étranger*, was sentenced to death for a murder he committed which he could only explain by rambling on about 'the glitter of the Algerian sun'. This motiveless murder, hotly discussed across the world, brought Camus and his novel attention, helping him win the Nobel Prize in 1957. Our Lord Asunaro, too, would no doubt have put things down to the sun by declaring that everything was owing to the fine weather and the fact that the world was at peace. One was a fictional character, the other historical, but both were monstrous in their own way.

In his favour it could be said that Asunaro was childishly artless, and lived a life that was, as it were, without deceit. Why have I chosen to chronicle an unimpressive person such as him? It is because in him I saw someone rare for his time, a modern man, no, a *normal* man, someone who became what anyone in his situation – a life of leisure, deprived of the means of doing anything truly fruitful (aside from the fruit engendered by his 'penchant') – would become. In other words, a man like you or me.

Afterword

In writing this I am greatly indebted to the information contained in the writings of historians and renowned readers of ancient texts. If I make a point of emphasising here that a considerable amount of the above is of course fiction, it is from a perhaps over-fussy fear that I may have distorted the facts found in these books, or denigrated the real persons who appear in the story (who of course have descendants alive today). Please keep in mind that the protagonist of this tale, despite being a real historical figure, inhabits what is essentially an imaginary world. With apologies...

Kanji Hanawa
translated by Meredith McKinney

'I have admired the Akutagawa Prize-nominated Hanawa's literary style for a long time. Each time he is nominated, I recommend him. And I am delighted that he continues to write at the same prize-winning level.'

Shohei Ooka, novelist and winner of the Mystery Writers of Japan Award, as well as the Noma, Asahi and Yomiuri Prizes

'He writes with a surreal style, similar to how I do on occasion, which I find very interesting and stimulating. But what makes me really happy is that he does it so much better than I do.'

Makoto Shiina, author of *Gaku Monogatari*

'Coping with expectations and finding our place in the world is something even Japanese warlords have known to struggle with. This is a samurai story with a difference – an amusing and compelling yarn concerning the discovery of one's passions and legacy. All good storytelling can be read as a metaphor for something, and this thought-provoking tale by Kanji Hanawa is no exception.'

Alex Pearl, author of *Sleeping with the Blackbirds*

'…is an important work of social commentary doing what all the greatest short stories do: opening a rabbit hole of thought down which the reader will fall.'

***The Japan Times*, commenting on *Backlight* by Kanji Hanawa**

'At short novella-length, *Backlight* is a quick story – but quite effective at raising interesting questions, including about cultural and social differences and attitudes, and parental responsibilities… the universal issues and questions it addresses give it the air of larger work'.

***The Complete Review*, commenting on *Backlight* by Kanji Hanawa**

Red Circle Minis

Original, Short and Compelling Reads

Red Circle Minis is a series of short captivating books by Japan's finest contemporary writers that brings the narratives and voices of Japan together as never before. Each book is a first edition written specifically for the series and is being published in English first.

The book covers in the series draw on traditional Japanese motifs and colours found in Japanese building, paper, garden and textile design. Everything, in fact, that is beautiful and refined, from kimonos to zen gardens and everything in between. The mark included on the covers incorporates the Japanese character *mame* meaning 'bean', a word that has many uses and connotations including all things miniature and adorable. The colour used on this cover is known as *umegasane*.

 Red Circle

Showcasing Japan's Best Creative Writing

Red Circle Authors Limited is a specialist publishing company that publishes the works of a carefully selected and curated group of leading contemporary Japanese authors.

For more information on Red Circle, Japanese literature, and Red Circle authors, please visit:
www.redcircleauthors.com